KU-477-161

Kit Williams

I have words to offer wisdom
And pictures to delight,
A story of a tragic Queen
And a fearless knight.
But my name remains a secret
It's hidden here within,
If you can but find it
More treasure you might win.

JONATHAN CAPE
THIRTY BEDFORD SQUARE LONDON

Ambrose the bee-keeper sat in his kitchen watching the last gleam of evening sunshine come through the little stained glass window in his back door. As the shadows lengthened into dusk he let his cat Trafalgar out into the chill darkness of the Spring night. He closed the damper on the stove and stoked up the fire. Then Ambrose plodded wearily up the narrow staircase to his bedroom. Once in bed he fell into a heavy sleep.

Outside, as the stars floated like tiny grains of pollen on the surface of a deep, black lake, the four seasons came together to ponder an age-old riddle:

> *Is each season born*
> *Out of the season that came before,*
> *Or will each in its turn*
> *Kill and conquer its forebear?*

Standing tall and pale, Autumn delivered a long speech about the birthright of Kings, ending with the words, "The King is dead, long live the King." To his right stood Spring, who felt a slight stirring within her but said nothing. Winter, white and waxen, for whom the flowers refuse to open, gathered his shroud about him and said gravely, "Death is my servant, rattling at your door. Who could be born again of these old bones?"

Only Summer was not there in person. He had sent his lion and his lion-keeper, a fat baby-faced dwarf with greedy little hands who swaggered about with the lion on a leash squeaking, "Summer izz as Summer duzz." The seasons argued long and hard and as they did so, dawn broke on the first day of Summer.

The first day of Summer is also the last of Spring. There was a freshness in the air as the misty veils of night receded.

As the light strengthened, to illuminate the honey-tinted world beneath the surface of a still, woodland pool, pale sunbeams slipped unnoticed through the swordsmen in the rushes to drink the dewy beads of quicksilver gathered on the lily-pads.

Later, when morning had put on her fine petticoats of green and yellow, there came others, dressed in smart velvet and black satin. They, too, stopped to sip at the gleaming droplets.

Without a city there is a house
That's made entire of wood,
Where live ten thousand daughters
That work for a common good.
One mother hath these daughters
And on her wedding day,
She became a widow
And royal sisters did she slay.

The sun rose into the sky and spread its warmth all about and the citizens grew restless to be abroad.

ot far from the pool, at the edge of the wood, stood an ancient tree, naked and hunched. Generations of small birds had nested in its knot-holes and many an owl had slept away its days blinking and contented in the camouflage of leaves and branches. Hedgehogs passed the winter snug in a wrapping of warm leaves beneath the twisted roots, and later brought forth whole families like little nail-brushes to snuffle and jostle in the undergrowth. Brightly coloured lichen speckled the aged bole and a host of happy-go-lucky plants found a home round the mossy base. The rabbits that lived in galleries below came out flirting their tails to nibble the fresh green shoots along the hedgerow.

But from one of the branches a bird swung in the still air, not as a herald to the change in the weather, but dead, head down and broken. The rook had been put there by a gamekeeper as a black warning to all who passed by, as if the chilled bones of Winter himself had been left to hang on these crooked gallows.

Heedless of such warnings Spring stepped out into the sunlit meadow and delighted in the touch of the dew between her toes. Among the grasses countless wild flowers grew, each eager to show its face. Strange and compelling patterns in mauve and violet enticed the bees to enter in and inside every flower there were precious jewels fashioned in curious colours with perfect geometry.

Put jet beads inside a poppy
Or topaz in the rue,
Loan dead nettle a carnelian,
Lend the scilla sapphires blue,
Endow loosestrife with jade of clouded green,
Now fill willow-herb with turquoise, treasure for a Queen.

While Spring busied herself among the wild flowers, a creature stole into the meadow. Wary at first but debonair at heart, he was soon chasing the butterflies that played hide-and-seek in the long grasses. He was a smart dandy of a young lion, with brightly polished teeth and newly sharpened claws. He had the most terrifying roar because that very morning he had eaten the whole of the London Symphony Orchestra for breakfast, instruments and all.

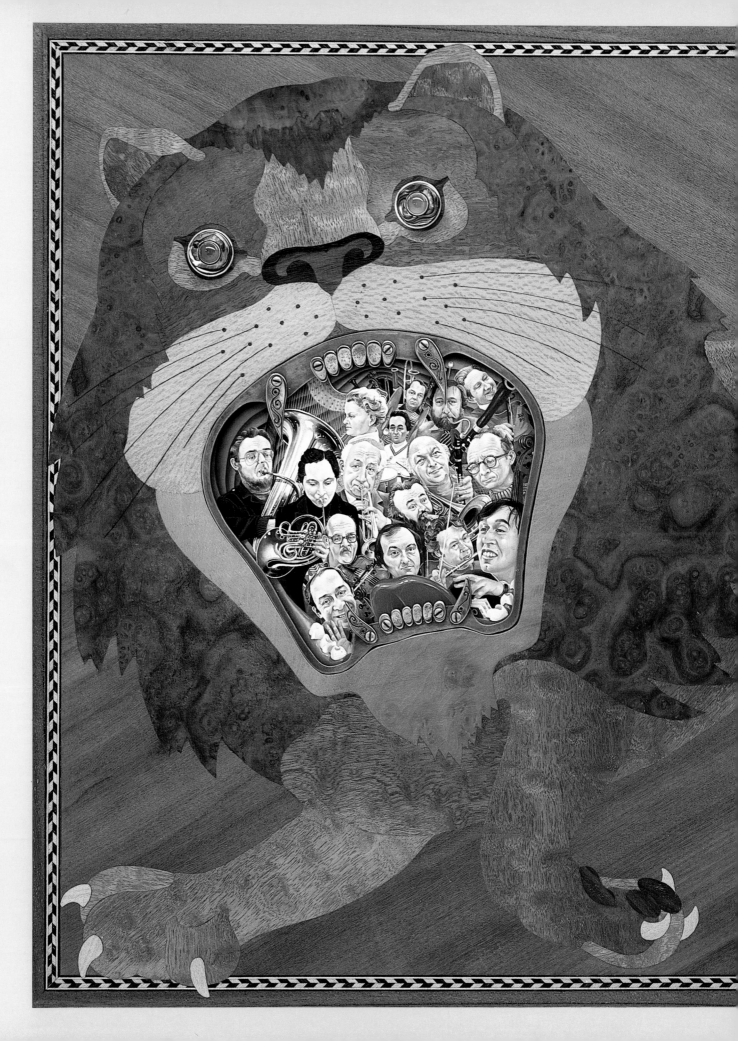

The fat little lion-keeper heard the roaring and rushed to the cage only to find his charge had escaped. He stamped and raged and cursed, kicking over the feed bucket in his fury. Then he grabbed his whip and his lion-taming chair and rushed out into the countryside.

When he came within sight of the enchanted meadow there was a sudden cooling of the air and the sky darkened as cloud heaped upon cloud. For Summer, who had put on his Great Bronzen Helmet and taken up his dreadful sword, mounted the shadowy horse of destiny and rode out upon the land.

Whipped by the restless wind and lashed by sudden rain, the lion-keeper ran as fast as his little legs could carry him to escape the wrath of Summer for allowing his charge to go free. "Summer uzz as Summer dizz," he panted, but it was too late. The iron hooves of Summer's war-horse thundered across the sky and the flashing of his armour lit up the distant hills. Bending in the saddle, Summer reached down and with pitiless savagery plucked off the dwarfish head and threw it screaming over the mountain tops.

The wind and the rain abated and out of the storm there came forth sweetness. Two swallows swooped and banked in the clearing sky and Spring hastened from the meadow. There were a thousand and one little last-minute jobs yet to be done. Some primroses had wantonly seeded themselves in the footpath and needed transplanting. There were nests to be inspected, with eggs of every description still waiting to be speckled. Chrysalises had to be woken and their stays loosened. Ladybirds required spotting and all manner of greedy little grubs were waiting to be fed. Besides this, the kitchen gardens and herbaceous borders had not been weeded. Vetch must be seeded, bindweed potted on, sowthistle scattered, and the carrot rows studded with leather-jackets. So much, so much to do!

The lion, bored with chasing butterflies, slept for a while. When he awoke he felt hungry and looked around for something to eat, but there was nothing. Then he smelt the faintest whiff of mouse. With whiskers twitching, he followed the scent through the undergrowth. But the mouse had heard the clumsy creature; it hesitated for a moment and then leapt to safety.

Finding a secure foothold, the mouse clung on and hid among the folds of Spring's dress. Unaware of the drama, Spring stood up and slowly walked along the path to the wood.

The urgency of the past months was over. The wood seemed to be drawing her towards it and in it she saw the closeness of her hour. She remembered the brave snowdrops that had defied the icy winds, and the sweet violets and celandines that had set the birds a-singing. She thought of wood anemones, the wind-flowers waving in the coppice, and jack-by-the-hedge and little germander speedwell. They had all, in their time, lightened her labour and now the ramsons and bluebells, campion and kingcup, ox-eye and cuckoo-pint rejoiced in the coming of …

One swallow cannot make me
Nor the gentian blue,
But see a rose and you will know
That I am good and true.

The lion had followed Spring at a safe distance, still in pursuit of his quarry. Then, circling around and putting himself in exactly the right position, he crouched low. His eyes got bigger and bigger, then Spring … was over. In catching the mouse the lion had killed frail Spring. And yet, as she lay in the grass, all Summer's flowers grew up out of her and shone in the morning sun.

A thin shaft of sunlight stood absolutely still as it pierced the silent dimness of a cottage bedroom.

As the earth revolved, the cottage moved and so too the bedroom until the thin white beam lit up the edge of a wooden bed. Slowly, imperceptibly, the world rotated and inch by inch the many contours of the counterpane were illuminated. Tiny specks of dust sparkled in the sunbeam as it gently penetrated the dreams of the sleeping man. Ambrose woke up, yawned and stretched, then, swinging his legs out of bed, he sat up and slipped his feet into a pair of worn carpet slippers. He slowly crossed the room, half knelt on a chair and opened the curtains.

The first day of Summer flooded into the room all ablaze with glorious colour and heavy with the scent of countless blooms. Ripples of birdsong broke the silence and Ambrose, filling his lungs with the eager breath of the morning, all but burst with excitement. He flung on his clothes and clattered down the stairs.

mbrose's little kitchen was as warm and cosy as fresh baked bread. He went to the stove and opened the damper, riddled the ashpit with a poker and moved the kettle on to the hotplate. Straight away it began to sing and in no time was boiling. Half of the water he poured into an enamel saucepan to boil an egg and, after warming the pot, made tea with the rest. While the egg boiled and the tea brewed, Ambrose cut slices of bread and hunks of cheese. He packed them with an apple, and a pickled onion wrapped in greaseproof paper, into a small tin lunch-box. When four minutes had passed on the mantel clock, Ambrose retrieved the egg with a large spoon and popped it into an egg-cup. He was about to tap the top when he was surprised to hear a curious scratching sound. Putting his ear to the shell he listened closely and realised that it wasn't the egg at all, but Trafalgar, the cat, scratching at the back door to be let in. Ambrose filled a dish with milk and placed it in front of the stove, then went to open the door. Without looking up, Trafalgar went straight to the milk. He drank thirstily, lapping and purring at the same time.

The man looked at the cat; no comfy creature of the hearthrug was this but a hunter of the night. It finished its milk and stretched. The man thoughtfully continued his meal.

After breakfast Ambrose picked up the lunch-box and went out into the porch. He placed his bee veil and smoker, along with a half flagon of cider, in a cardboard box and tied it on his bicycle. As he bent to put on his cycle clips he noticed a small mouse lying dead on the flagstones. He picked it up and looked closer. Into his mind came the thought of a pretty lady in a russet gown curled up and fast asleep in the palm of his hand. He went out of the house, sadly carrying the mouse in one hand and pushing the bicycle with the other. The bicycle bumped down the steps and at the bottom he leant it against the railings. Ambrose placed the mouse under a laurel bush. "Why do cats kill for pleasure?" he pondered as he returned to the bicycle.

As he mounted to set off he noticed the flowers. Every few yards a freshly picked daisy lay abandoned in the road. But by whom? And to what end? He started looking out for them, steering as close as he could without actually running them over and his heart lightened as the daisy chase made him swerve this way and that all along the road. The game continued and whichever turning he had to take, the flowers mysteriously went that way too, as if he were being led to some magical encounter. Faster and faster he pedalled and to each daisy he shouted a jovial greeting. He found himself cycling with ease up hills that in the past had defeated him and, as the countryside sped by, he thought he heard the distant roar of cheering.

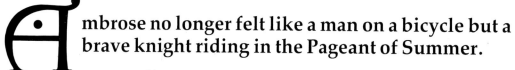mbrose no longer felt like a man on a bicycle but a brave knight riding in the Pageant of Summer.

All in the blue, unclouded weather
With helmet and helmet feather,
On burnished hoof for love and fame
To bear aloft the oriflamme.

Reaching his destination, the noble Ambrose dismounted. As he laid his trusty steed to rest on a grassy bank, he noticed a tortoiseshell comb lying in the grass, at the end of a chain of daisies. Contemplating the beautiful ornament made Ambrose wonder if two lovers had met by moonlight and in the shadows let it fall. Or had it been shaken loose during the laughing capers of a family picnic? Would its mistress return in the hope of finding it, or had she already accepted the loss? As he stooped to pick it up he hesitated, imagining the joy such a comb would bring to the face of a village girl who might chance upon it. He thrilled at the thought of being the sole keeper of the secret, and withdrew his hand.

Cloistered in a wooden tower, a forlorn Queen toiled in honeyed darkness. For her there were no sunny days among the flowers, just the corridors and chambers of a dim labyrinth. To ease the pains of her labours she dreamed: "One day a prince will come to free me from this endless twilight and the waiting and the weeping will be over."

The hive was in a sheltered place away from wind and the trampling of sheep and cattle. There were trees close by that gave cool shade and served as a resting place for swarms. Ambrose prepared his equipment for opening the hive. He lit the smoker, gave it a few trial puffs and then proceeded with the task. Deftly, Ambrose applied a little smoke to the entrance and waited until he heard the deep, busy murmur of the workers gorging themselves with honey. Satisfied that they were subdued by their activities, he bent down to lift up the roof. It was the first time the hive had been opened this year and Ambrose was anxious to know how well the colony had survived Winter.

A dizziness of blue exploded into the golden shades of the city. The citizens scrambled in turmoil over the wooden ramparts, appalled by the dreadful violation. Methodically the bee-keeper dismantled the city piece by piece, inspecting every frame until he found the Queen. He stopped to admire her youth and royal splendour, then carefully reassembled the hive, well pleased with what he had seen. The citizens returned to their allotted labours and the Queen to her dreams. For it may be said that although the ways of men are many and varied, to the bees they are of little consequence.

As Ambrose straightened up he thought he heard a faint murmur from within the hive:

"Summer izz as Summer duzz."

For L·E·B·

by the same author
MASQUERADE

First published 1984
Copyright © 1984 by Kit Williams

Jonathan Cape Ltd, 30 Bedford Square, London WC1

British Library Cataloguing in Publication Data

Williams, Kit
[Untitled children's story]
823'.914[J]   PZ7
ISBN 0-224-01906-6

Conditions of sale
This book is sold subject to the condition
that the Plates therein, or any part of
them, shall not, by way of trade or
otherwise, be made up for sale, or resold
in any form other than the form in which
they are published.

Printed in Italy by A. Mondadori Editore, Verona